HORRiD HENRY
and the
Zombie Vampire

Francesca Simon
Illustrated by Tony Ross

Orion
Children's Books

ORION CHILDREN'S BOOKS

First published in Great Britain in 2011 by Orion Children's Books
This edition published in 2015 by Hodder and Stoughton

18

Text © Francesca Simon, 2011
Illustrations © Tony Ross, 2011

A CIP catalogue record for this book
is available from the British Library.

ISBN 978 1 84255 135 6

Printed and bound in Great Britain by
Clays Ltd, St Ives plc

The paper and board used in this book are
made from wood from responsible sources.

MIX
Paper from
responsible sources
FSC® C104740

Orion Children's Books
An imprint of
Hachette Children's Group
Part of Hodder & Stoughton
Carmelite House
50 Victoria Embankment
London EC4Y 0DZ

An Hachette UK Company
www.hachette.co.uk

www.hachettechildrens.co.uk
www.horridhenry.co.uk

For the amazing, inspiring, and fantastic
Josh Stamp-Simon

CONTENTS

1

HORRID HENRY WRITES A STORY

'NO!' screamed Horrid Henry. 'NO!'

'Don't be horrid, Henry,' said Dad.

'We'd LOVE to hear your new story, Peter,' said Mum.

'I wouldn't,' said Henry.

'Don't be rude, Henry,' said Dad.

Horrid Henry stuck his fingers in his ears and glared.

AAAARRRRRGGGGHHHHH.

Wasn't it bad enough that he had to sit at the table in front of a disgusting plate filled with – yuck – sprouts and – blecccchh – peas instead of the chips

1

and pizza he had BEGGED Dad to cook for dinner? Did he really have to listen to Peter droning on as well?

This was torture. This was a cruel and unusual punishment. Did any child in the world ever suffer as much as Henry?

It was so unfair! Mum and Dad wouldn't let him play the Killer Boy Rats during dinner but now they wanted to force him to listen to Peter read his stupid story.

Peter wrote the world's worst stories. If they weren't about fairies, they were about kittens, or butterflies, or little elves that helped humans with their chores. His last one was all about the stupid adventures of Peter's favourite plastic sheep, Fluff Puff, and the terrible day his  pink and yellow nose turned blue. The king of the sheep had to come and wave his magic hoof to change it back . . .

2

Henry shuddered just remembering. And then Henry had shouted that a woodsman who really fancied a lamb chop had nabbed Fluff Puff and then Mum and Dad had sent him to his room.

Perfect Peter unfolded his piece of paper and cleared his throat.

'My story is called, *Butterfly Fairies Paint the Rainbow*,' said Peter.

'AARRGGHHH!' said Henry.

'What a lovely title,' said Mum. She glared at Henry.

3

'Can't wait to hear it,' said Dad.
'Stop playing with your food, Henry,'
he added, as Horrid Henry started
squishing peas under his knife.

'Once upon a time there lived seven
butterfly fairies. There was one for
every colour of the rainbow. Dance
and prance, prance and dance, went the
butterfly fairies every day.'

Henry groaned. 'That's just copying
Daffy and her Dancing Daisies.'

'I'm not copying,' said Perfect Peter.

'Are too.'

'Am not.'

'Don't be horrid, Henry,' said Mum.
'Peter, that's a lovely story so far. Go
on, what happens next?'

'The butterfly fairies also kept the
rainbow lovely and shiny. Each fairy
polished their own colour every day.
But one day the butterfly fairies looked

4

up at the sky. Whoopsydaisy! All the colours had fallen off the rainbow.'

'Call the police,' said Horrid Henry.

'Mum, Henry keeps interrupting me,' wailed Peter.

'Stop it, Henry,' said Mum.

'The fairies ran to tell their queen what had happened,' read Peter.

'"All the colours of the rainbow fell down," cried the butterfly fairies.

"Oh no."

"Oh woe."

"Boo hoo. Boo hoo.'"

SCRATCH! SCRAPE!

Horrid Henry started grinding his knife into his plate.

'Stop that, Henry,' said Dad.

'I'm just eating my dinner,' said Henry. He sighed loudly. 'You're always telling me to use my knife. And now I am and you tell me to stop.'

Perfect Peter raised his voice. "'Don't cry, butterfly fairies," said the Queen. "We'll just—'"

SCRAPE!

Horrid Henry scraped louder.

'Mum!' wailed Peter. 'He's trying to ruin my story.'

'There's nothing to ruin,' said Henry.

'Be quiet, Henry,' said Dad. 'I don't want to hear another word out of you.'

6

Henry burped.

'Henry! I'm warning you!'

'I didn't *say* anything,' said Henry.

'Mum! I'm just getting to the really exciting bit,' said Peter. 'Henry's spoiling it.'

'Go on Peter, we're all listening,' said Mum.

'"Don't cry, butterflies," said the Queen. "We'll just have to pick up our magic paint pots and colour it back in."

"Yay," said the fairies. "Let's get to work."'

'Blecchhhhhhh!' said Horrid Henry, pretending to vomit and knocking a few sprouts onto the floor.

'Henry, I'm warning you . . . ' said Mum. 'Sorry, Peter.'

'"I'll paint the rainbow blue," said blue butterfly.

"I'll paint the rainbow orange," said

7

orange butterfly.

"I'll paint the rainbow green," said green butterfly.

"I'll paint—"'

'"I'll paint the rainbow black and hang skulls on it,"

said Terminator butterfly,' snarled Horrid Henry. 'MUM!' wailed Peter. 'Henry's interrupting me *again*!'

'Henry, this is your final warning,' said Dad. 'If I hear one more word out of you, no TV for a week.'

'Then the Fairy Queen picked up the paint pots and—'

Horrid Henry yawned loudly.

' . . . and the butterfly fairies were so happy that they began to sing:

"Tee hee. Tra la.

Tra la tra la

We are dainty little fairies

And we play and sing all day

Maybe you can come and join us

Then we'll paint the day away

Tee hee hee hee

Tra la la la."'

'Blah blah, blah blah,' snarled Horrid Henry. He hadn't thought Peter could write a worse story than *The Adventures of Fluff Puff* but he was wrong.

'That's the worst story I ever heard,' said Horrid Henry.

'Henry. Be quiet,' said Dad.

Horrid Henry's fingers curled around a sprout.

'What did *you* think of my story, Mum?' said Peter.

9

'That was the best story I ever heard,' said Mum.

'Well done Peter,' said Dad.

Bong! A sprout hit Perfect Peter on the head.

'OW! Henry just threw a sprout at me,' wailed Peter.

'Didn't!' said Henry. 'It slipped off my fork.'

'That's it, Henry!' shouted Dad.

'Go to your room, Henry!' shouted Mum.

Horrid Henry leapt down from the table and began to stomp. 'Look at me, I'm a butterfly fairy!'

Horrid Henry stomped upstairs to his bedroom. It was so unfair. In the olden days, when people hadn't enjoyed a play, didn't they throw tomatoes and rotten oranges at the stage? He was only being historical.

Peter was lucky he
hadn't thrown much
worse at him.
Well, he'd
show everyone
how it was
done.
He'd
write the
greatest
story ever.

All about King Hairy the Horrible
and his wicked
wife Queen
Gertrude the
Gruesome.

They would
spend their
days cackling
and making evil plans.

Horrid Henry lay down on his bed.

11

He'd get writing as soon as he finished this week's *Screamin' Demon* comic.

'Margaret! Stop shouting!
  Steven! Stop grunting!
  William! Stop weeping!
  Soraya! Stop singing!
  Henry! Just stop!
  Everyone. BE QUIET!' yelled Miss Battle-Axe. She mopped her brow. One day she would retire to a war zone and enjoy the peace and quiet.

Until then . . . she glared at her class.

'Now. I want everyone to settle down and write a story.'

Horrid Henry scowled. Miss Battle-Axe always hated his stories, even Henry's brilliant one about the Troll Werewolf Mummies who hid beneath teachers' beds and snacked on their toes. She hadn't even liked his cannibal can-can story about the cannibal dance troupe who ate their way across Europe.

It was hard, heavy work writing a story. Why should he bother when his efforts met with so little reward?

What was that stupid thing Peter had read out last night? That would do. Quickly Horrid Henry scribbled down Peter's dreadful Butterfly Fairies story. Miss

Battle-Axe didn't deserve anything better.

Done! Now back to his comic.
Screamin' Demon was just about to
discover where the Master of the
Macabre had hidden the treasure . . .

Horrid Henry felt a long fingernail
poke into his shoulder. He looked up
into Miss Battle-Axe's evil eye.

' . . . and why aren't you writing your
story, Henry?' hissed Miss Battle-Axe.

Horrid Henry smiled.

'Because I've finished it,' said Henry.

'You . . . finished it?' said Miss Battle-
Axe. She tugged on her ear. Perhaps it
was time she had her earwax removed
again.

'Yup,' said Henry.

'Let me see,' said Miss Battle-Axe,
holding out her bony claw.

Tee hee, thought Horrid Henry,
handing her the story. She doesn't

believe me. Wouldn't batty old Miss
Battle-Axe get a surprise.

'Hmmm,' said Miss Battle-Axe
after she'd finished reading. 'Hmmm.
Butterfly Fairies Paint the Rainbow.
Hmmm.' She stared at Henry and tried
to smile but her mouth had trouble
turning up due to lack of practice.
'*Much* better than usual, Henry.'

Henry stared. The men in white coats
would be coming to take Miss Battle-
Axe away any moment if she liked this
story better than his others.

'In fact . . . in fact . . . I want you to
go now to Miss Lovely's class and read it
out loud to the Infants. They'll love it.'
What? NO!!!!!!!

Perfect Peter's class sat expectantly on
the carpet as Horrid Henry stood before
them, story in hand. Now everyone

would think *he'd* written this stupid story. Moody Margaret would tease him until he was old and grey and toothless. But what could he do? He was trapped.

'*Putter fair pat the rainb* . . . ' mumbled Horrid Henry.

'Speak up, Henry,' said Miss Lovely. 'Don't be shy. We're *so* looking forward to your story.'

'*Butterfly Fairies Paint the Rainbow,*' hissed Horrid Henry.

Perfect Peter's jaw dropped. Too late Henry realised his mistake. Writing a story about butterfly fairies was bad enough. But he'd never hear the end of it if people found out he'd *copied* his younger brother's story. Though even Peter wouldn't be such a tell-tale . . . would he?

Peter put his hand in the air.

'Miss Lovely, that's *my*—' began Peter.

16

'Just kidding,' said Horrid Henry
hastily. 'My story is really called, uh,
Butterfly Fairies Fight the Giants.'

He glanced down at his story,
changing words as he read:

'Once upon a time there lived two
hideous giants, King Hairy the Horrible
and Queen Gertrude the Gruesome.
Stamp and stomp, stomp and stamp
went the hideous giants every day.

They liked stomping on fairies,

17

especially the butterfly fairies who polished the rainbow every day.

One day the giants looked up at the sky. Whoopsydaisy! All the butterfly fairies had fallen off the rainbow.

"Oh what fun," cackled King Hairy the Horrible, squishing the blue butterfly fairy.

"Yippee!" squealed Queen Gertrude the Gruesome, squashing the orange butterfly fairy.

"Ha ha!" they both shrieked, stomping on the green butterfly fairy.'

Perky Parveen looked shocked.

Spotless Sam began to sniff.

"'I'm going to roast those fairies for dinner," said Queen Gertrude the Gruesome. "Yum, yum!" she drooled, as the delicious smell of cooked fairy wafted through the castle kitchen. Then the Queen picked up the fairy bones and—'

Miss Lovely looked pale.

Oh no, what now, thought Horrid Henry desperately. He'd reached Peter's horrible fairy song.

"Tee hee. Tra la.

Tra la tra la

We are dainty little fairies

And we play and sing all day

Maybe you can come and join us

Then we'll paint the day away

Tee hee hee hee

Tra la la la."

Horrid Henry took a deep breath.

'King Hairy the Horrible and Queen Gertrude the Gruesome were so happy that they began to sing:

"Tee hee. Ha ha. Ha ha ha ha.
We are big and ugly giants
And we belch and kill all day
Maybe we can come and find you
Then we'll squish your guts away
Tee hee tee hee
Ha ha ha ha,"

bellowed Horrid Henry.

Perky Parveen began to cry.

'The fairwies got squished,' sobbed Lisping Lily.

'I don't want the giants to eat the fairies,' shrieked Tidy Ted.

'I'm scared,' howled Helpful Hari.

'I want my Mama,' wept Needy Neil.

'Wah!' wailed the Infants.

Horrid Henry was thrilled. What a reaction! Maybe I'll add a bit more,

thought Horrid Henry. This is such a great story it's a shame to end it here.

'Let's find some bunnies,' snarled the giants. 'I'm sure—'

'Stop! Stop!' said Miss Lovely. She looked ashen. 'Better go back to your class,' she whispered. What had Miss Battle-Axe been thinking?

Horrid Henry shook his head and closed the door on the screaming, howling class.

Wow. What a great story he'd written.

Maybe he should be an author when he grew up.

2

HORRiD HENRY AND
THE NUDIE FOODIE

'Children, I have some *thrilling* news,'
burbled Mrs Oddbod.

Horrid Henry groaned. His idea of
thrilling news and Mrs Oddbod's idea
of thrilling news were not the same.
Thrilling news would be Mutant
Max replacing Mrs Oddbod as head.
Thrilling news would be Miss Battle-
Axe being whisked off to ancient Rome
to be a gladiator. Thrilling news would
be Moody Margaret dumped in a
swamp and Perfect Peter sent to prison.

Thrilling news wasn't new coat hooks and who was in the Good as Gold book.

But wait. What was Mrs Oddbod saying? 'Our school has been chosen to be a healthy-eating school. Our new healthy and nutritious school meals will be an example for schools everywhere.'

Horrid Henry sat up. What? *Healthy* eating? Oh no.

Henry

knew what grown-ups meant by healthy food. Celery. Beetroot. Aubergine towers. Anything that tasted yucky and looked

24

revolting was bound
to be good for him.
Anything that tasted
yummy was bound
to be bad. Henry had plenty of healthy
eating at home. Was
nowhere safe?

'And guess
who's going to
help make our

school a beacon of
healthy eating?' babbled
Mrs Oddbod. 'Only
the world-famous chef,
Mr Nudie Foodie.'

Rude Ralph snorted. 'Nudie,'
he jeered.

Mr Nudie Foodie? thought
Horrid Henry. What kind of
stupid name was that? Were
there really parents out there

whose surname was Foodie, who'd
decided that the perfect name for their
son was Nudie?

'And here he is, in person,'
proclaimed Mrs Oddbod.

The children clapped as a shaggy-
haired man wearing a red-checked
apron and a chef's hat bounced to the
front of the auditorium.

'From today your school will be *the* place for delicious, nutritious food,' he beamed. 'I'm not nude, it's my food that's nude! My delicious, yummalicious grub is just plain scrummy.'

Horrid Henry couldn't believe his ears. Just plain, delicious food? Why, that was *exactly* what Horrid Henry loved. Plain burgers. Plain pizzas just with cheese and nothing else. No sneaky flabby pieces of aubergine or grisly chunks of red pepper ruining the topping. Plain chips slathered in ketchup. No funny bits. No strange green stuff. Three cheers to more burgers, more chips and more pizza!

Horrid Henry could see it now. Obviously, *he'd* be asked to create the yummy new school menu of plain, delicious food.

Monday: crisps, chips, ice cream, cake, burgers

Tuesday: burgers, chips, crisps, chocolate

Wednesday: pizza, chips, crisps, ice cream

Thursday: chocolate cake

Friday: burgers, pizza, chips, crisps, cake, ice cream

(after all, it was the end of the week, and nice to celebrate). Oh, and fizzywizz drinks every day, and chocolate milk. There! A lovely, healthy, plain, nutritious and delicious menu that everyone would love. Because, let's face it, at the moment school dinners *were* horrid. They only served burgers and chips once a week,

thought Horrid Henry indignantly.
Well, he'd soon sort *that* out.

In fact, maybe *he* should be a famous
chef when he got older. Chef Henry,
the burger wizard. Happy Henry,
hamburger hero. He would open a
chain of famous restaurants, called
*Henry's! Where the eatin' can't be
beaten!* Hmmm, well, he'd have
time to improve the name, while
collecting his millions every week
from the restaurant tills
as happy customers
fought their way
inside for the chance
to chow down
on one of Happy

Henry's bun-tastic
burgers. Kids
everywhere
would beg to

29

eat there, safe in the knowledge that no vegetables would ever contaminate their food. Ahhh! Horrid Henry sighed.

Mr Nudie Foodie was leaping up and down with excitement. 'And you're all going to help me make the delicious food that will be a joy to eat. Remember, just like the words to my hit song:

It's not rude
To be a dude
Who loves nude food.
Yee haw.'

'Well, Nudie,' said Mrs Oddbod. 'Uhh, I mean, Mr Foodie . . . '

'Just call me Mr Nudie Foodie,' said Mr Nudie Foodie. 'Now, who wants to be a nudie foodie and join me in the kitchen to make lunch today?'

'Me!' shouted Perfect Peter.

'Me!' shouted Clever Clare.

'I want to be a nudie foodie,' said Jolly Josh.

'I want to be a nudie foodie,' said Tidy Ted.

'I want to be a nudie foodie,' yelled Greedy Graham. 'I think.'

'A healthy school is a happy school,' said Mr Nudie Foodie, beaming. 'My motto is: Only bad food boos, when you choose yummy food. And at lunchtime today, all your parents will be coming to the cafeteria to sample our scrumptious, yummalicious, fabulicious and irresistible new food! Olé!'

Horrid Henry looked round the school kitchen. He'd never seen so many pots and pans and vats and cauldrons. So this was where the school glop was made.

31

Well, not any longer. Would they be making giant whopper burgers in the huge frying pans? Or vats and vats of chips in the huge pots? Maybe they'd make pizzas for the gigantic ovens!

The Nudie Foodie stood before Henry's class. 'This is so exciting,' he said bouncing up and down. 'Everyone ready to make some delicious food?'

'Yes!' bellowed Henry's class.

'Right, then, let's get cooking,' said Mr Nudie Foodie.

Horrid Henry stood in front of a chopping board with Weepy William, Dizzy Dave and Fiery Fiona. Fiery Fiona shoved Henry.

'Stop hogging the chopping board,' she hissed.

 Horrid Henry shoved her back, knocking the

lumpy bag of ingredients onto the floor.

'Stop hogging it yourself,' he hissed back.

'Wah!' wailed Weepy William.

'Henry pushed me.'

Wait. What was rolling all over the floor? It looked like . . . it couldn't be . . .

'Group 1, here's how to slice a yummy green pepper,' beamed Mr Nudie Foodie. 'And Group 2, you're in charge of the tomatoes . . . Group 3, you make the broccoli salad. Group 4 will look after the mushrooms.'

Green pepper? Tomatoes? Broccoli? Mushrooms? What was this muck?

33

'It's my yummy, scrummy, super, secret, vege-tastic pasta sauce!' said Mr Nudie Foodie.

What? What a dirty rotten trick. Where were the chips? Where were the burgers?

And then suddenly Horrid Henry understood Mr Nudie Foodie's evil plan. He was going to sneak *vegetables* onto the school menu. Not just a single vegetable, but loads and loads and loads of vegetables. Enough evil vegetables to kill someone a hundred times over. Boy impaled by killer carrot.

Girl chokes to death on deadly broccoli. Boy gags on toxic tomato. Henry could see the headlines now.

They'd find him dead in the lunchroom, poisoned by vegetables, his limbs twisted in agony . . .

Well, *no way*. No way was this foul fiend going to trick Henry into eating vegetables.

Everyone chopped and stirred and mixed. The evil brew hissed and

bubbled. Horrid Henry had never felt so cheated in his life.

Finally, the bell rang.

Mr Nudie Foodie stood by the exit with an enormous black bin bag.

'Before you leave I want you to open your lunch boxes and dump all your junk food in here. No need for that stuff today.'

'Huh?' said Rude Ralph.

'No!' wailed Greedy Graham.

'Yes!' said Mr Nudie Foodie. 'You'll thank me later.'

Horrid Henry gasped in horror as everyone threw their yummy snacks into the bag as they filed out of the kitchen and ran out for playtime. For once Henry was glad his mean, horrible parents never packed anything good in *his* lunchbox.

Was there no end to this evil man's plots? thought Horrid Henry, stomping past Mr Nudie Foodie into the hall. First, vegetable pasta sauce, then stealing everyone's sweets? What a waste. All those treats going straight into the bin . . .

'Rescue us Henry!' squealed the chocolate and crisps trapped inside the bin bag. 'Help!'

Horrid Henry didn't need to be asked twice. He crept down the hall and darted back into the school kitchen.

Sweets, here I come, thought Horrid Henry.

The kitchen was empty. Huge vats of vegetable sauce sat ready to be poured onto pasta. What horrors would Mr Nudie Foodie try to sneak on the menu tomorrow? And the next day? And the next? Just wait until the parents discovered the sauce was made of vegetables. They'd make the children eat this swill every day.

AAAAARRRRRGGGHHHHH. And then suddenly Horrid Henry knew what he had to do. He looked longingly at the enormous black bin bag bulging with crisps and chocolate  and yummy snacks. Horrid Henry gritted his teeth. Sometimes you had to think ahead. Sometimes you couldn't be distracted. Not even by doughnuts.

There wasn't a moment to lose. Any second a teacher or dinner lady could come in and foil him. He had to seize his chance to stop Mr Nudie Foodie once and for all.

Grabbing whatever was nearest, Horrid Henry emptied a tin of salt into the first vat of sauce. Into the second went a tin of mustard powder. Into the third went a bottle of vinegar. Into the fourth and final one . . .

Henry looked at the gurgling, bubbling, poisonous, reeking, rancid, toxic sauce. Take that, Nudie Foodie, thought Horrid

40

Henry, reaching for a tub of lard.

'What are you doing, Henry?' rasped a deadly voice.

Henry froze.

'Just looking for my lunchbox,' he said, pretending to search behind the cooking pots.

Miss Battle-Axe snarled, flashing her yellow brick teeth. She pointed to the door. Horrid Henry ran out.

Phew. What a lucky escape. Shame he hadn't completed his mission, but three vats out of four wasn't bad. Anyway, the fourth pot was sure to be disgusting, even without extra dollops of lard.

You are dead meat, Mr Nudie Foodie, thought Horrid Henry.

'Parents, children, prepare yourselves for a taste sensation!' said Mr Nudie Foodie, ladling out pasta and sauce.

Lazy Linda's mother took a big forkful. 'Hmm, doesn't this look yummy!' she said. 'It's about time this school served proper food,' said Moody Margaret's mum, shovelling an enormous spoonful into her mouth.

'I couldn't agree more,' said Tidy Ted's dad, scooping up pasta.

'BLECCCCHHHHH!' spluttered Margaret's mother, spitting it out all over Aerobic Al's Dad. Her face was

42

purple. 'That's disgusting! My Maggie Moo-Moo won't be touching a drop of that!'

'What are you trying to do, poison people?!' screamed Aerobic Al's Dad. His face was green.

'I'm not eating this muck!' shouted Clever Clare's Mum. 'And Clare certainly isn't.'

'But . . . but . . .' gasped Mr Nudie Foodie. 'This sauce is my speciality, it's delicious, it's—' he took a mouthful.

'Uggghhhh,' he said, spewing it all over Mrs Oddbod. 'It *is* disgusting.'

Wow, thought Horrid Henry. Wow. Could the sauce really be *so* bad? He had to try it. Would he get the salty, the mustardy, the vinegary, or just the plain disgusting vegetably?

Henry picked up a tiny forkful of pasta, put it in his mouth and swallowed.

He was still breathing. He was still alive. Everyone at his table was slurping up the food and beaming. Everyone at the other tables was coughing and choking and spitting . . .

Horrid Henry took another teeny tiny taste.

The sauce was . . . delicious. It was much nicer than the regular glop they served at lunchtime with pasta. It was a million billion times nicer. And he had just . . . he had just . . .

'Is this some kind of joke?' gasped Mrs Oddbod, gagging. 'Mr Nudie Foodie,

44

you are toast! Leave here at once!'

Mr Nudie Foodie slunk off.

'NOOOOO!' screamed Horrid Henry. 'It's yummy! Don't go!'

Everyone stared at Horrid Henry.

'Weird,' said Rude Ralph.

3

HORRID HENRY AND THE MAD PROFESSOR

Horrid Henry grabbed the top secret
sweet tin he kept hidden under his bed.
It was jampacked with all his favourites:
Big Boppers. Nose Pickers. Dirt Balls.
Hot Snot. Gooey Chewies. Scrunchy
Munchies.

Yummy!!!

Hmmm boy! Horrid Henry's
mouth watered as he prised off the lid.
Which to have first? A Dirt Ball? Or a
Gooey Chewy? Actually, he'd just scoff
the lot. It had been ages since he'd . . .

Huh?

Where were all his chocolates? Where were all his sweets? Who'd nicked them? Had Margaret invaded his room? Had Peter sneaked in? How dare—Oh. Horrid Henry suddenly remembered. *He'd* eaten them all.

Rats.

Rats.

Triple rats.

Well, he'd just have to go and buy more. He was sure to have loads of pocket money left.

Chocolate, here I come, thought Horrid Henry, heaving his bones and dashing over to his skeleton bank.

 He shook it. Then he shook it again.

There wasn't even a rattle.

How could he have *no* money and
no sweets? It was so unfair! Just last
night Peter had been boasting about
having £7.48 pence in *his* piggy bank.
And loads of sweets left over from
Hallowe'en. Horrid Henry scowled.
Why did Peter *always* have money?
Why did he, Henry, *never* have money?

Money was totally wasted on Peter.
What was the point of Peter having
pocket money since he never spent it?
Come to think of it, what was the point
of Peter having sweets since he never
ate them?

There was a shuffling, scuttling noise,
then Perfect Peter dribbled into Henry's
bedroom carrying all his soft toys.

'Get out of my room, worm!'
bellowed Horrid Henry, holding his
nose. 'You're stinking it up.'

'I am not,' said Peter.

'Are too, smelly pants.'

'I do not have smelly pants,' said
Peter.

'Do too, woofy, poofy, pongy pants.'

Peter opened his mouth, then closed it.

'Henry, will you play with me?' said
Peter.

'No.'

'Please?'

'No!'

'Pretty please?'

'No!!'

'But we could play school with all my cuddly toys,' said Peter. 'Or have a tea party with them . . . '

'For the last time, NOOOOOOO!' screamed Horrid Henry.

'You *never* play with me,' said Perfect Peter.

'That's 'cause you're a toad-faced nappy wibble bibble,' said Horrid Henry. 'Now go away and leave me alone.'

'Mum! Henry's calling me names again!' screamed Peter. 'He called me wibble bibble.'

'Henry! Don't be horrid!' shouted Mum.

'I'm not being horrid, Peter's annoying me!' yelled Henry.

'Henry's annoying *me*!' yelled Peter.

'Make him stop!' screamed Henry and Peter.

Mum ran into the room.

'Boys. If you can't play nicely then leave each other alone,' said Mum.

'Henry won't play with me,' wailed Peter. 'He *never* plays with me.'

'Henry! Why can't you play with your brother?' said Mum. 'When I was little Ruby and I played beautifully together all the time.'

Horrid Henry scowled.

'Because he's a wormy worm,' said Henry.

'Mum! Henry just called me a wormy worm,' wailed Peter.

'Don't call your brother names,' said Mum.

'Peter only wants to play stupid baby games,' said Henry.

'I do not,' said Peter.

'If you're not going to play together then you can do your chores,' said Mum.

'I've done mine,' said Peter. 'I fed Fluffy, cleaned out the litter tray *and* tidied my room.'

Mum beamed. 'Peter, *you* are the best boy in the world.'

Horrid Henry scowled. He'd been far too busy reading his comics to empty the wastepaper bins and tidy his room.

He stuck out his tongue at Peter behind
Mum's back.

'Henry's making horrible faces at me,'
said Peter.

'Henry, *please* be nice for once and
play with Peter,' said Mum. She sighed
and left the room.

Henry glared at Peter.

Peter glared at Henry.

Horrid Henry was about to push
Peter out the door when suddenly
he had a brilliant, spectacular idea.
It was so brilliant and so spectacular
that Horrid Henry couldn't believe
he was still standing in his bedroom
and hadn't blasted off into outer space
trailing clouds of glory. Why had he
never thought of this before? It was
magnificent. It was genius. One day
he would start Henry's Genius Shop,
where people would pay a million

pounds to buy his super fantastic ideas.
But until then . . .

'Okay Peter, I'll play with you,' said
Horrid Henry. He smiled sweetly.

Perfect Peter could hardly believe his
ears.

'You'll . . . *play* with me?' said Perfect
Peter.

'Sure,' said Horrid Henry.

'What do you want to play?' asked Peter cautiously. The last time Peter could remember Henry playing with him they'd played Cannibals and Dinner. Peter had had to be dinner . . .

'Let's play Robot and Mad Professor,' said Henry.

'Okay,' said Perfect Peter. Wow. That sounded a lot more exciting than his usual favourite game – writing lists of

vegetables or having ladybird tea parties
with his stuffed toys. He'd probably
have to be the robot, and do what
Henry said, but it would be worth it,
to play such a fun game.

'I'll be the robot,' said Horrid Henry.

Peter's jaw dropped.

'Go on,' said Henry. 'You're the mad
professor. Tell me what to do.'

Wow. Henry was even letting *him* be
the mad professor! Maybe he'd been
wrong about Henry . . .
maybe Henry had been
struck by lightning
and changed into a
nice brother . . .

'Robot,' ordered
Perfect Peter. 'March around the room.'

Horrid Henry didn't budge.

'Robot!' said Peter. 'I order you to
march.'

'Pro—fes—sor! I— need—twenty-five p—to— move,' said Henry in a robotic voice. 'Twenty-five p. Twenty-five p. Twenty-five p.'

'Twenty-five p?' said Peter.

'That's the rules of Robot and Mad Professor,' said Henry, shrugging.

'Okay Henry,' said Peter, rummaging in his bank. He handed Henry twenty-five p.

Yes! thought Horrid Henry.

Horrid Henry took a few stiff steps, then slowed down and stopped.

'More,' said robotic Henry. 'More. My batteries have run down. More.'

Perfect Peter handed over another

twenty-five p.

Henry lurched around for a few
more steps, crashed into the wall and
collapsed on the floor.

'I need sweets to get up,' said the
robot. 'Fetch me sweets. Systems
overload. Sweets. Sweets. Sweets.'

Perfect Peter dropped two sweets into
Henry's hand. Henry twitched his foot.

'More,' said the robot. 'Lots more.'

Perfect Peter dropped four more

sweets. Henry jerked up into a sitting position.

'I will now tell you my top secret—secret—secret—secret—' stuttered Horrid Henry. 'Cross—my—palm—with—silver and sweets . . . ' He held out his robot hands. Peter filled them.

Tee hee.

'I want to be the robot now,' said Peter.

'Okay, robot,' said Henry. 'Run upstairs and empty all the waste-paper baskets. Bet you can't do it in thirty seconds.'

'Yes I can,' said Peter.

'Nah, you're too rusty and puny,' said Horrid Henry.

'Am not,' said Peter.

'Then prove it, robot,' said Henry.

'But aren't you going to give me—' faltered Peter.

'MOVE!' bellowed Henry. 'They don't call me the MAD professor for nothing!!!'

Playing Robot and Mad Professor was a bit less fun than Peter had anticipated. Somehow, his piggy bank was now empty and Henry's skeleton bank was full. And somehow most of Peter's Hallowe'en sweets were now in Henry's sweet box.

Robot and Mad Professor was the most fun Henry had ever had playing with Peter. Now that he had all Peter's money and all Peter's sweets, could he trick Peter into doing all his chores as well?

'Let's play school,' said Peter. That would be safe. There was no way Henry could trick him playing *that* . . . .

'I've got a better idea,' said Henry. 'Let's play Slaves and Masters. You're the slave. I order you to . . . '

'No,' interrupted Peter. 'I don't want to.' Henry couldn't make him.

'Okay,' said Henry. 'We can play school. You can be the tidy monitor.'

Oh! Peter loved being tidy monitor.

'We're going to play Clean Up The Classroom!' said Henry. 'The classroom is in here. So, get to work.'

Peter looked around the great mess of toys and dirty clothes and comics

and empty wrappers scattered all over Henry's room.

'I thought we'd start by taking the register,' said Peter.

'Nah,' said Henry. 'That's the baby way to play school. You have to start by tidying the classroom. You're the tidy monitor.'

'What are you?' said Peter.

'The teacher, of course,' said Henry.

'Can I be the teacher next?' said Peter.

'Sure,' said Henry. 'We'll swap after you finish your job.'

Henry lay on his bed and read his comic and stuffed the rest of Peter's sweets into his mouth. Peter tidied.

Ah, this was the life.

'It's very quiet in here,' said Mum, popping her head round the door. 'What's going on?'

'Nothing,' said Horrid Henry.

'Why is Peter tidying your room?' said Mum.

''Cause he's the tidy monitor,' said Henry.

Perfect Peter burst into tears. 'Henry's taken all my money and all my sweets and made me do all his chores,' he wailed.

'Henry!' shouted Mum. 'You horrid boy!'

★

On the bad side, Mum made Henry
give Peter back all his money. But on
the good side, all his chores were done
for the week. And he couldn't give
Peter back his sweets because he'd
eaten them all.

Result!

4

· ·

HORRID HENRY
AND THE ZOMBIE
VAMPIRE

'Isn't it exciting, Henry?' said Perfect
Peter, packing Bunnykins carefully in
his Sammy the Snail overnight bag.
'A museum sleepover! With a torch-lit
trail! And worksheets! I can't think of
anything more fun.'

'I can,' snarled Horrid Henry.
Being trapped in a cave with Clever
Clare reciting all the multiplication
tables from one to a million. Watching
Cooking Cuties. Even visiting Nurse
Needle for one of her horrible

injections. (Well, maybe not *that*).

But *almost* anything would be better than being stuck overnight in Our Town Museum on a class sleepover. No TV. No computers. No comics. Why oh why did he have to do this? He wanted to sleep in his own comfy bed, not in a sleeping bag on the museum's cold hard floor, surrounded by photos of old mayors and a few dusty exhibits.

AAARRRRGGGHH. Wasn't it bad enough he was bored all day in school without being bored all night too?

Worse, Peter's nappy baby class was coming, too. They'd probably have to be tucked in at seven o'clock, when they'd all start crying for their mamas. Ugghh. And

68

then Miss Battle-Axe snarling at them
to finish their worksheets, and Moody
Margaret snoring and Anxious Andrew
whimpering that he'd seen a ghost . . .

Well, no way was he going to that
boring old dump without some comics
to pass the time. He'd just bought the
latest *Screamin' Demon* with a big article
all about vampires and zombies. Yay!
He couldn't wait to read it.

Perfect Peter watched
him stuff his Mutant
Max bag full of
comics.

'Henry, you know
we're not allowed to
bring comics to the
museum sleepover,' said
Perfect Peter.

'Shut up and mind your own business,
toad,' said Horrid Henry.

69

'Mum! Henry just called me a toad!' wailed Peter. 'And he told me to shut up.'

'Toady Toady Toady, Toady Toady Toady,' jeered Henry.

'Henry! Stop being horrid or no museum sleepover for you,' yelled Mum.

Horrid Henry paused. Was it too late to be horrid enough to get banned from the sleepover? Why hadn't he thought of this before? Why, he could . . .

'Henry! Peter! We have to leave *now!*' yelled Dad.

Rats.

The children queued up in the museum's Central Hall clutching their sleeping bags as Miss Lovely and Miss Battle-Axe ticked off names on a big register.

'Go away, Susan,' said Moody Margaret. 'After what you did at my

house I'm going to sit with Gurinder.
So there.'

'You're such a meanie, Margaret,' said
Sour Susan.

'Am not.'

'Are too.'

Susan scowled. Margaret was *always* so
mean. If only she could think of a way
to pay that old grouch back.

Margaret scowled. Susan was *always* so annoying. If only she could think of a way to pay that old fraidy cat back.

Henry scowled. Why did he have to be here? What he'd give for a magic carpet to whisk him straight home to the comfy black chair to watch *Terminator Gladiator*. Could life get any worse?

'Henwy,' came a little voice next to him. 'I love you Henwy. I want to give you a big kiss.'

Oh no, thought Horrid Henry. Oh no. It was Lisping Lily, New Nick's little sister. What was that foul fiend doing here?

'You keep away from me,' said Horrid Henry, pushing and shoving his way through the children to escape her.

'Waaa!' wept Weepy William as Henry stepped on his foot.

'I want my mama,' cried Needy Neil as Henry trampled on his sleeping bag.

'But I want to marry with you, Henwy,' lisped Lily, trying to follow him.

'Henry! Stay still!' barked Miss Battle-Axe, glaring at him with her demon eyes.

'Hello boys and girls, what an adventure we're going to have tonight,' said the museum's guide, Earnest Ella, as she handed out pencils and worksheets.

Henry groaned. Boring! He hated worksheets.

'Did you know that our museum has a famous collection of balls of wool through the ages?' droned Earnest Ella. 'And an old railway car? Oh yes, it's going to be an exciting sleepover night. We're even going on a torch-lit walk through the corridors.'

Horrid Henry yawned and sneaked a peek at his comic book, which he'd hidden beneath his museum worksheet.

Watch out, Demon Fans!! To celebrate the release of this season's big blockbuster monster horror film, **THE ZOMBIE VAMPIRES**, study this check-list. Make sure there are no zombie-vampires lurking in your neighbourhood!!!!

Horrid Henry gasped as he read *How To Recognise a Vampire* and *How to Recognise a Zombie*. Big scary teeth?

Big googly eyes? Looks like the walking dead? Wow, that described Miss Battle-Axe perfectly. All they had to add was big fat carrot nose and . . .

A dark shadow loomed over him.

'I'll take that,' snapped Miss Battle-Axe, yanking the comic out of his hand. '*And* the rest.'

Huh?

He'd been so careful. How had she spotted that comic under his worksheet?

And how did she know about the secret stash in his bag? Horrid Henry looked round the hall. Aha! There was Peter, pretending not to look at him. How dare that wormy worm toad tell on him? Just for that . . .

'Come along everyone, line up to collect your torches for our spooky walk,' said Earnest Ella. 'You wouldn't want to get left behind in the dark, would you?'

There was no time to lose. Horrid Henry slipped over to Peter's class and joined him in line with Tidy Ted and Goody Goody Gordon.

'Hello Peter,' said Henry sweetly.

Peter looked at him nervously. Did Henry suspect *he'd* told on him? Henry didn't *look* angry.

'Shame my comic got confiscated,' said Henry, ''cause it had a list of how

76

to tell whether anyone you know is a zombie vampire.'

'A zombie vampire?' said Tidy Ted.

'Yup,' said Henry.

'They're imaginary,' said Goody-Goody Gordon.

'That's what they'd *like* you to believe,' said Henry. 'But I've discovered some.'

'Where?' said Ted.

Horrid Henry looked around dramatically, then dropped his voice to a whisper.

'Two teachers at our school,' hissed Henry.

'Two *teachers?*' said Peter.

'What?' said Ted.

'You heard me. Zombie vampires. Miss Battle-Axe *and* Miss Lovely.'

'Miss *Lovely*?' gasped Peter.

'You're just making that up,' said Gordon.

'It was all in *Screamin' Demon*,' said Henry. 'That's why Miss Battle-Axe snatched my comic. To stop me finding out the truth. Listen carefully.'

Henry recited:

'How to recognise a vampire:
1. BIG HUGE SCARY TEETH.'

'If Miss Battle-Axe's fangs were any bigger she would trip over them,' said Horrid Henry.

Tidy Ted nodded. 'She *does* have big pointy teeth.'

'That doesn't prove anything,' said Peter.

'2. DRINKS BLOOD.'

Perfect Peter shook his head. 'Drinks . . . blood?'

'*Obviously* they do, just not *in front* of people,' said Horrid Henry. 'That would give away their terrible secret.'

'3. ONLY APPEARS AT NIGHT.'

'But Henry,' said Goody-Goody Gordon, 'we see Miss Battle-Axe and Miss Lovely every day at school. They *can't* be vampires.'

Henry sighed. 'Have you been paying attention? I didn't say they were *vampires*, I said they were *zombie* vampires. Being half-zombie lets them walk about in daylight.'

Perfect Peter and Goody-Goody Gordon looked at one another.

'Here's the total proof,' Henry continued.

'How to recognise a zombie: 1. LOOKS DEAD.'

'Does Miss Battle-Axe look dead? Definitely,' said Horrid Henry. 'I never saw a more dead-looking person.'

'But Henry,' said Peter. 'She's alive.'

Unfortunately, yes, thought Horrid Henry.

'Duh,' he said. 'Zombies always *seem* alive. Plus, zombies have got scary, bulging eyes like Miss Battle-Axe,' continued Henry. 'And they feed on human flesh.'

'Miss Lovely doesn't eat human flesh,' said Peter. 'She's a vegetarian.'

'A likely story,' said Henry.

'You're just trying to scare us,' said Peter.

'Don't you see?' said Henry. 'They're planning to pounce on us during the torch-lit trail.'

'I don't believe you,' said Peter.

Henry shrugged. 'Fine. Don't believe me. Just don't say I didn't warn you when Miss Lovely lurches out of the dark and BITES you!' he shrieked.

'Be quiet, Henry,' shouted Miss Battle-Axe. 'William. Stop weeping.

There's nothing to be scared of. Linda! Stand up. It's not bedtime yet. Bert! Where's your torch?'

'I dunno,' said Beefy Bert.

Miss Lovely walked over and smiled at Peter.

'Looking forward to the torchlit walk?' she beamed.

Peter couldn't stop himself sneaking a peek at her teeth. *Were* they big? And sharp? Funny, he'd never noticed before how pointy two of them were . . . And was her face a bit . . . umm . . . pale?

No! Henry was just trying to trick him. Well, he wasn't going to be fooled.

'Time to go exploring,' said Earnest Ella. 'First stop on the torch-lit trail: our brand-new exhibit, *Wonderful World of Wool*. Then we'll be popping next door down the *Passage to the Past* to visit the old railway car and the Victorian shop

and a Neanderthal cave. Torches on, everyone.'

Sour Susan smiled to herself. She'd just thought of the perfect revenge on Margaret for teasing her for being such a scaredy cat.

Moody Margaret smiled to herself. She'd just thought of the perfect revenge on Susan for being so sour.

Ha ha Margaret, thought Susan. I'll get you tonight.

Ha ha Susan, thought Margaret. I'll get you tonight.

Ha ha Peter, thought Henry. I'll get you tonight.

'Follow me,' said Earnest Ella.

The children stampeded after her.

All except three.

When the coast was clear, Moody Margaret turned off her torch, darted into the pitch-black *Passage to the Past* hall and hid in the Neanderthal cave behind the caveman. She'd leap out at Susan when she walked past. MWAHAHAHAHAHAHA! Wouldn't that old scaredy cat get a fright.

Sour Susan turned off her torch and peeked down the *Passage to the Past* corridor. Empty. She tiptoed to the railway car and crept inside. Just wait till Margaret walked by . . .

Horrid Henry turned off his torch, crept down the *Passage to the Past*, sneaked into the Victorian shop and hid behind the rocking chair.

Tee hee. Just wait till Peter walked past. He'd—

What was that?

Was it his imagination? Or did that spinning wheel in the corner of the shop . . . move?

CR—EEEK went the wheel.

It was so dark. But Henry didn't dare switch on his torch.

Moody Margaret looked over from the Neanderthal cave at the Victorian shop. Was it her  imagination or was that rocking chair rocking back and forth?

Sour Susan looked out from the railway car. Was it her imagination or was the caveman moving?

There was a strange, scuttling noise.

What was that? thought Susan.

You know, thought Henry, this museum *is* kind of creepy at night.

And then something grabbed onto his leg.

'AAAARRRRGGHHH!' screamed Horrid Henry.

Moody Margaret heard a blood-curdling scream. Scarcely daring to breathe, Margaret peeped over the caveman's shoulder . . .

Sour Susan heard a blood-curdling scream. Scarcely daring to breathe, Susan peeped out from the railway carriage . . .

'Henwy, I found you, Henwy,' piped the creature clinging to his leg.

'Go away Lily,' hissed Henry. The horrible fiend was going to ruin everything.

'Will you marry me, Henwy?'

'No!' said Horrid Henry, trying to shake her off and brushing against the spinning wheel.

CR—EEEEK.

The spinning wheel spun.

What's that noise? thought Margaret, craning to see from behind the caveman.

'Henwy! I want to give you a big kiss,' lisped Lily.

Horrid Henry shook his leg harder.

The spinning wheel tottered and fell over.

CRASH!

Margaret and Susan saw something lurch out of the Victorian shop and loom up in the darkness. A monstrous creature with four legs and waving arms . . .

'AAAARRRRGGHH!' screamed Susan.

'AAAARGGHHHHH!' shrieked Margaret.

'AAAARGGHHHHH!' shrieked
Henry.

The unearthly screams rang through the
museum. Peter, Ted, and Gordon froze.

'You don't think—' gasped Gordon.

'Not . . . ' trembled Peter.

'Zombie vampires?' whimpered Ted.
They clutched one another.

'Everyone head back to the Central
Hall NOW!' shouted Earnest Ella.

★

In the cafeteria, Miss Lovely and Miss Battle-Axe were snatching a short break to enjoy a lovely fried egg sandwich with lashings of ketchup.

Oh my weary bones, thought Miss Battle-Axe, as she sank her teeth into the huge sandwich. Peace at last.

AAARRGGHH! EEEEEKKK! HELLLP!

Miss Battle-Axe and Miss Lovely squeezed their sandwiches in shock as they heard the terrible screams.

SPLAT!

A stream of ketchup squirted Miss Lovely in the eye and dripped down her face onto her blouse.

SQUIRT!

A blob of ketchup splatted Miss Battle-Axe on the nose and dribbled down her chin onto her cardigan.

'Sorry, Boudicca,' said Miss Lovely.

'Sorry, Lydia,' said Miss Battle-Axe.

They raced into the dark Central Hall just as their classes ran back from the torch-lit walk. Fifty beams of light from fifty torches lit up the teachers' ketchup-covered faces and ketchup-stained clothes.

'AAAARRGGHHH!' screamed Perfect Peter.

'It's the zombie vampires!' howled Tidy Ted.

'Run for your lives!' yelped Goody-Goody Gordon.

'Wait!' shouted Miss Lovely! 'Children, come back!'

'We won't eat you!' shouted Miss Battle-Axe.

'AAAARRRRGGHHHHHH!'

ACKNOWLEDGEMENTS

Jenny Gyertson has had her lovely story
Fairies Paint the Rainbow *stolen*
not once but twice: the least she deserves
is an acknowledgement.

My thanks also to Steven Butler
for telling me all about Theft Number One . . .

HORRiD HENRY BOOKS

Horrid Henry
Horrid Henry and the Secret Club
Horrid Henry Tricks the Tooth Fairy
Horrid Henry's Nits
Horrid Henry Gets Rich Quick
Horrid Henry's Haunted House
Horrid Henry and the Mummy's Curse
Horrid Henry's Revenge
Horrid Henry and the Bogey Babysitter
Horrid Henry's Stinkbomb
Horrid Henry's Underpants
Horrid Henry Meets the Queen
Horrid Henry and the Mega-Mean Time Machine
Horrid Henry and the Football Fiend
Horrid Henry's Christmas Cracker
Horrid Henry and the Abominable Snowman
Horrid Henry Robs the Bank
Horrid Henry Wakes the Dead
Horrid Henry Rocks
Horrid Henry and the Zombie Vampire
Horrid Henry's Monster Movie
Horrid Henry's Krazy Ketchup
Horrid Henry's Cannibal Curse

Colour books

Horrid Henry's Big Bad Book
Horrid Henry's Wicked Ways
Horrid Henry's Evil Enemies
Horrid Henry Rules the World
Horrid Henry's Dreadful Deeds
Horrid Henry's House of Horrors
Horrid Henry Shows Who's Boss
Horrid Henry's Tricky Tricks

Horrid Henry is also available on CD and as a digital download, all read by Miranda Richardson.

"A hoot from beginning to end . . .
As always, Miranda Richardson's delivery is perfection and the manic music is a delight."
Daily Express

"Long may this dreadful boy continue to terrorise all who know him. He's a nightmare, but so entertaining . . . Miranda Richardson's spirited reading is accompanied by a brilliant music soundtrack – they make a noisy and fun-filled duo."
Parents' Guide

Also by Francesca Simon

HORRID HENRY

The first book about the adventures of Horrid
Henry, in which Henry tries (unbelievably) to
be good, goes to dance classes, makes 'Glop'
with Moody Margaret and goes on holiday.

'Henry is a truly
great character'
Sunday Times

HORRiD HENRY
Tricks the Tooth Fairy

Horrid Henry returns – and this time he tries
to trick the Tooth Fairy, sends Moody
Margaret packing, makes teachers run
screaming from school . . . and single-handedly
wrecks a wedding.

HORRID HENRY
and the
Mummy's Curse

Horrid Henry has a new hobby,
tries to avoid learning his spellings,
creates havoc at the swimming pool,
and convinces Peter to turn
Fluffy the cat into a mummy!

HORRiD HENRY
Gets Rich Quick

Horrid Henry makes sure he gets the presents
he wants for Christmas, sabotages the school
sports day, runs away from home, and thinks
of a brilliant way to get rich quick.

HORRiD HENRY
Robs the Bank

Horrid Henry helps himself to all the money he needs to win his favourite board game, comes up with another spectacular money-making scheme for launching a newspaper with all the school gossip, vows vengeance on Perfect Peter when Peter steals his birthday party theme and has his own Pirate Party, then takes over as Head Teacher when Peter plays school with his goody-goody friends.

HORRiD HENRY
Wakes the Dead

Horrid Henry
finds a sure-fire way of
wielding the remote control
to ensure he always watches his
programme of choice, vies with
Moody Margaret to become the head
of the school, shows off his prowess as
a magician in the school talent show, and
battles it out with Perfect Peter over who
gets the green dinosaur and who gets the
purple one.

HORRiD HENRY
Rocks

Horrid Henry and Perfect Peter keep
invading each other's rooms, Moody Margaret
invites the Secret Club for a sleepover, with
catastrophic results, Miss Battle-Axe's class have
to write their autobiographies, the best to be
published in the local paper, and Horrid Henry
wants to go to the Killer Boy Rats concert not
the Daffy and her Dancing Daisies concert –
what can Henry do?